Dear Parent:
Your child's love of reading starts here!

Every child learns to read in a different way and at his or her own speed. Some go back and forth between reading levels and read favorite books again and again. Others read through each level in order. You can help your young reader improve and become more confident by encouraging his or her own interests and abilities. From books your child reads with you to the first books he or she reads alone, there are I Can Read Books for every stage of reading:

SHARED READING
Basic language, word repetition, and whimsical illustrations, ideal for sharing with your emergent reader

BEGINNING READING
Short sentences, familiar words, and simple concepts for children eager to read on their own

READING WITH HELP
Engaging stories, longer sentences, and language play for developing readers

READING ALONE
Complex plots, challenging vocabulary, and high-interest topics for the independent reader

ADVANCED READING
Short paragraphs, chapters, and exciting themes for the perfect bridge to chapter books

I Can Read Books have introduced children to the joy of reading since 1957. Featuring award-winning authors and illustrators and a fabulous cast of beloved characters, I Can Read Books set the standard for beginning readers.

A lifetime of discovery begins with the magical words "I Can Read!"

Visit www.icanread.com for information
on enriching your child's reading experience.

I Can Read Book® is a trademark of HarperCollins Publishers.

Dixie and the Best Day Ever
www.icanread.com

Library of Congress catalog card number: 2013950467
ISBN 978-0-06-208661-7 (trade bdg.) —ISBN 978-0-06-208659-4 (pbk.)

14 15 16 17 18   SCP   10 9 8 7 6 5 4 3 2 1   ❖   First Edition

I Can Read!

BEGINNING 1 READING

Dixie

and the Best Day Ever

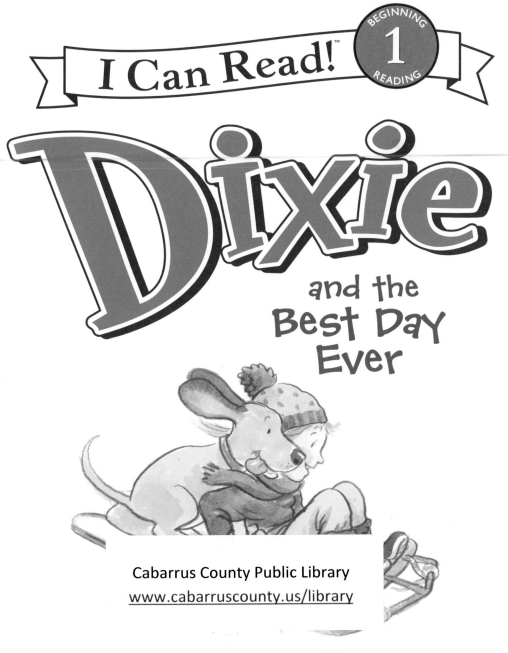

story by Grace Gilman
pictures by Jacqueline Rogers

HARPER

An Imprint of HarperCollinsPublishers

Emma had to write a poem

about her best day ever.

"I don't know what to write,"

she told Dixie.

Emma looked at the weather outside.

"We're going to have a snow day.

I just know it," said Emma.

"I can write my poem tomorrow."

The next day was a snow day!

"Let's play outside," said Emma.

Dixie shook her head.

She took Emma's notebook

off the table.

"I can write my poem later,"

explained Emma.

Emma ran outside.

She threw a snowball.

Dixie ran to fetch it.

She made paw prints in the snow.

Emma threw more snowballs.

Dixie tried to fetch them,

but they all fell apart.

"Let's make snow angels!"

said Emma.

Dixie didn't make a snow angel.

She ran off with Emma's scarf.

"Come back, Dixie!" called Emma.

Emma chased Dixie to the house.

"I'm not ready to go in yet,"

Emma said,

as she took her scarf back.

Dixie barked at two kids with sleds.

They were on their way to Big Hill.

"Let's go sledding, too!"

said Emma.

Emma got her sled.

"It's a snow day," said Emma.

"Let's have fun."

Big Hill was down the street,

just past the park.

Dixie ran next to Emma.

When they got to the park,

Dixie sniffed around the slide.

Then she started to dig.

Emma rolled big snowballs.

Dixie came over with two rocks,

a sock, and a stick.

"Ta-da!" said Emma.

She made a snow dog!

Dixie barked.

The snow dog looked just like her!

At last, they got to Big Hill.

Emma and Dixie started to climb.

Emma and Dixie huffed and puffed.

Big Hill was steep.

"We made it!" said Emma

when they got to the top.

She turned the sled.

She was ready to race!

But then Dixie jumped on the sled.

"Wait, Dixie!" said Emma.

It was too late.

Dixie was sledding down the hill.

Down, down, down Dixie went.

The sled picked up speed.

"Oh, no!" said Emma.

Dixie had never been

sledding alone before.

"Do you need a ride?" someone called.

It was Emma's friend Amy.

"Follow that dog," Emma said.

Emma jumped in the front.

"I'm coming, Dixie!" Emma called.

Their sled raced down the hill.

When Dixie saw Emma coming,

she left her sled and ran up the hill.

"No, Dixie!" called Emma.

"Get out of the way!"

Dixie did not listen to Emma.

She jumped into Emma's lap.

The sled bumped into a snow bank.

Everyone fell off, giggling.

"Let's do it again!" said Emma.

"I'll ride with Dixie this time."

Emma and Dixie sledded down Big Hill

again and again and again.

"I can do this all day," said Emma.

It was Dixie's turn to pull the sled

up the hill.

But this time, Dixie ran the other way.

Emma ran after Dixie.

Dixie knew where she was going.

Dixie was going home.

Emma had to write her poem.

"The best day ever . . . is today!"

Emma told Dixie.

Dixie wagged her tail,

and Emma wrote her poem.